The Very Secret Garden Shed

Written by Rebecca Clements

Illustrated by Gloria Vanessa Nicoli

Written by Rebecca Clements

Text copyright Rebecca Clements ©2021

Illustrated by Gloria Vanessa Nicoli

Illustrations Copyright Gloria Vanessa Nicoli ©2021

First Edition 2021

The Very Secret Garden Shed

ISBN : 978-1-8382938-6-4

For Jane

*M*r. Price has lived in his cottage in the quiet village of Winter Park for many years. A grumpy old man, Mr. Price did not enjoy gardening. Instead, he enjoyed reading the newspaper in the morning, watching the news each lunchtime whilst eating a cheese and pickle sandwich, and sipping hot cups of tea for the rest of the day whilst tackling a puzzle. Therefore, grumpy Mr. Price's garden was overgrown, full of brambles, and was home to many creatures like spiders, beetles, worms, and birds.

Mr. Price's garden was also home to another family. At the very bottom of the garden, through the long grass, past the blackberry bush, and through the rotting wooden archway that once was covered in beautiful roses, was a garden shed.

The shed looked very much like any other old shed. Resting against its side was a rusty spade, and the once-clear windows looking in were now cracked and filled with cobwebs. Whilst it looked very ordinary, this shed was most unusual indeed, and held an important secret, for it was the South Regional Sorting Office for the National Tooth Fairy Headquarters, based in the Tooth Fairy Kingdom.

The regional sorting offices, based all over the world—came in many different forms. Some were bandstands in giant parks, other entrances were hidden through red letterboxes in stoned walls, and others were simply in hollows of trees in peaceful woods. It would cause a mighty traffic jam for all the tooth fairies in the world to fly to the kingdom each night to deliver their teeth, and so the secret sorting offices provided a great way for the fairies to collect the teeth to make sure they are all healthy and clean before dropping them off to the kingdom, to be made into shining white castles and crowns.

*I*t was the most normal and ordinary day when the news came into the South Regional Sorting Office via a field mouse that lived in the garden.

"Wake up, wake up, wakeup!" said the panicked field mouse to the sleeping fairies, who spent a large part of the day sleeping after their nightly rounds of teeth collecting.

"What is it, Jasper? It's still daylight," said Juliet grumpily. Juliet was a fiery fairy with fierce red hair and a fairy skirt that looked like flames when she spun around.

"Mr. Price is selling his house!" said Jasper, who was a rather nervous mouse, anyway, spluttering in an all-out panic now.

The news had all three fairies up and awake straight away.

"Whatever do you mean? This can't be right," Scarlet, with her long brown hair, said as she flew up to look out of the window of the shed. Scarlet was of a cooler, calmer demeanour, who's fairy skirt appeared to be made of water.

5

Sure enough, Scarlet could see right through the kitchen window and into the small front garden that now had a very large, very red "for sale" sign blowing softly in the spring breeze.

"Jasper, call an urgent meeting with the garden creatures. Have everyone meet us here in one hour and ask the ants to find out what's going on. The ants know everything," said Agatha. The oldest and wisest of the fairies, Aggie, as her friends called her, always had a plan when needed. Aggie's wisdom made her the more grounded and down-to-earth fairy of the trio, and her fairy skirt was made of moss and leaves.

*O*ne hour later, nestled between plant pots, old seed trays, and rusting tools, the garden creatures gathered. The fairies sat at the front and, after a whispered conversation with the queen ant, Aggie stepped forward.

"Mr. Price has decided to move to Spain and spend the rest of his retirement in the sunshine. The ants heard him on the phone, talking to his friend Dave. The house is to be sold."

There were gasps from the garden creatures, but the real worry came from Scarlet and Juliet, who had a very important job as tooth fairies to the boys and girls of Winter Park. They had worked ever so hard to make the shed a perfect sorting office and home. They loved their job very much and the thought of the old shed being pulled down by new owners was a very big problem. It would take an age to find a new home and set everything up again. The poor boys and girls who lost teeth in that time would be left with them and nothing in reward for all the hard work they spent brushing and taking care of them.

The next few weeks passed quickly with lots of unusual folks trapesing through Mr. Price's house and into the garden. Luckily, because of the long grass, nettles, and brambles, the shed stayed hidden, and Aggie, Scarlet, and Juliet carried on with their important tooth fairy duties.

The fairies had amazing powers and could see well into a person's heart; they could hear the heartbeat and even read some thoughts. This enabled the fairies to tell if those who'd come were virtuous and kind or if they were maleficent, bound to harm all those small creatures living in the garden.

*M*r. Price was not asking a fortune in exchange for his old house and, for that reason, countless young couples and families inspected the property until, eventually, the Smiths looked like they were close to purchasing it.

Their grumpy nature and teen boy, who looked rather bitter with a dark aura around him, spelled trouble.

Scarlet and the other fairies, along with the mice and the beetles, were watching the scene, hidden in the tall grasses and shrubs.

The horror in their eyes was visible, as Mrs. Smith was already boasting about her plans to tear everything down, even the trees, to build a pool with a minibar. Her arms were flowing in all directions now as the little heads of the fairies followed each move with grief.

"Oh no, she is going to destroy our home!" Aggie sobbed along with all the other creatures.

At first, they felt powerless, especially since the Smiths had the money and looked determined to buy Mr. Price's house.

The smile on the old man's face as he was thinking about the money he was going to get in exchange had nothing in common with the fairies' sorrow.

They looked with frozen eyes at how their livelihoods would soon be ruined, after so long; the shed might have fallen in disrepair, but it was their home, and all that vegetation provided shade and food for all those little animals.

Soon, it would all be gone!

*J*uliet, whose feisty nature did not allow her to give up so easily, came with a burst of courage.

"We need to do something about it! We can't let those devious people buy Mr. Price's house!"

The other fairies looked at their friend in utter disbelief.

"What can we do? Mr. Price can sell his house to whoever he wants. It's not in our power to prevent it," Aggie muttered with a sad look on her face.

A quick council with all the animals in the back yard was formed; birds, mice, lizards, beetles, and dragonflies, plus others, attended.

Juliet came up with a daring plan now.

"We can spook them off and wait until the right family comes by!"

There was little faith in this plan, but they all agreed to participate as there was no other hope left.

18

*T*he fairies went in first as the Smiths approached the grasses to inspect the property in detail; they spread their magic dust, causing them all to sneeze.

Billy, their teen boy, suffered the most, as he was allergic to pollen; he was out of breath as the mice began running around their feet, scaring the living soul out of them.

"Oh no! There are evil creatures here!" Poor Billy gasped in between sneezes.

The birds were flying over their heads, threatening to attack. It was a full-out war where the fairies and all the other creatures were throwing all they had at the devious family.

Mr. Price was in awe witnessing the assault as the bugs were crawling up their legs.

"What on earth is going on?!" He sighed, fixing his large glasses up on his nose.

"We need to get out of this hell, honey. This place is haunted!" Mrs. Smith cried out, urging her husband and boy to leave.

"Thanks, but no thanks. This house is not right for us. This jungle frightens me!" the woman added, almost running away.

Victory!

"*I* can't believe that worked," Aggie gasped. Their happiness could hardly be described in words as they cheered and danced around the shed. Their home was safe for now, and waiting for the right hearts to come and buy it.

By midspring, the house was sold, and Mr. Price was jetting away to the sunshine.

Just the very next weekend, the Georges moved into the cottage. Now Mr. and Mrs. George loved to garden. They also had two children: Rose and Lily. Two children who had both lost some teeth...

"Oh, my toothpaste! I hoped they would buy it!" cried Juliet, swishing her fairy skirt around and sprinkling fairy dust everywhere! "I know them!"

"What are you talking about, Juju?" asked Scarlet, who was polishing teeth for the drop off to HQ

"The people who have moved in! I am Rose and Lily George's tooth fairy!" Juliet beamed.

"They are the loveliest and kindest children, and they always leave me a thank-you note, and so I always sprinkle extra fairy dust on them."

Aggie considered this. This was good news; kind people were always the best type. "Maybe we won't have to move after all?" Aggie asked hopefully. Although, fairies were never ever to show themselves to human children or grown-ups, so it would be quite difficult to ask them to stay. They could, however, leave clues.

As the Georges got to work tackling the garden, the fairies started to leave clues that they lived in the shed, like sprinkling fairy dust everywhere! Whilst the Georges got to work clearing brambles, the fairies tinkled about and hoped the wind would carry their sweet songs to the children's ears.

Over the next few weeks, the garden was transformed. The bushes, now cut back, revealed the stone pathways once again, and the flower beds started to bloom with a sea of colourful petals. Mr. George dug a pond and added a small fountain. Mrs. George restored the wooden archway, and the children hung up handmade birdfeeders on the tree branches. The garden creatures were delighted to have a new watering hole, some excellent new hiding spaces, and a whole host of new friends that the garden attracted. Rose and Lily even built a bug hotel out of sticks and rocks. They really were the kindest girls who loved nature.

*B*ut the best bit of all...Mr. and Mrs. George decided the shed was the perfect place to store Rose and Lily's bikes and garden toys. They decided to paint it, fix it up, and add some new windows and shelves. Mrs. George even made some curtains and added a light. They swept out all of the old cobwebs, dust, and dirt, and the shed became a rather beautiful den at the end of the garden, where Rose and Lily would seek shade to read books and colour when the sun was too hot.

Aggie, Juliet, and Scarlet were most relieved and felt so wonderfully thankful for their shed makeover. Mostly, they were certain that Rose and Lily had heard them and made sure the South Regional Headquarters were kept safe as can be, so the fairies could always collect the teeth from the children of Winter Park on time. Magical fairy dust can make people do things without even realising it sometimes!

For years to come, the fairies enjoyed their home and continued to work hard. Mr. Price was no longer grumpy in Spain, and the Georges created lots of special and fun memories in their home.

*M*aybe you have a large tree in your garden, or you live by a quiet post-box. Maybe you have a bandstand in your local park or a stream with a small nook in its walled sides. If you do, next time you are there, listen hard and see if you can hear the fairies polishing teeth or filling their bags with coins for the night rounds. There are secret sorting offices all over the country. The chances are, there is one just by you too.

THE END

Made in the USA
Columbia, SC
08 September 2021